Ticked Tock

a short story

Judy Lunsford

Copyright Information
*

Ticked Tock
*

Ticked Tock

a short story

Judy Lunsford

It was a morning like any other morning. The sun was coming up over the mountains and was catching in the rearview mirror as Wesley was driving towards the city.

He tried to avoid looking in his mirror because the sun was blindingly bright as it caught his eyes in the reflection. He didn't want to adjust the mirror because it took forever to get it back to where he liked it. So, he figured he would just avert his eyes until the sun was high enough that it was out of his rearview mirror's sight.

Wesley kept his eyes focused on the road ahead of him and tilted his head so that the sun's reflection wasn't in his eyes.

He focused on staying in his lane so he wouldn't need his mirror and jabbed a finger at the car radio to change the station. He normally liked to listen to the news while he was in the car because, as an artist that mostly worked from home, the car radio was his only connection to the outside world. But the news was too depressing for this kind of morning, so Wesley tried to find something more suitable for the long drive into the city.

He found a station that was playing old rock music and tried to sing along as he drove. He used to love singing in the car, but it had been a while since he had heard the song and found he didn't remember the words.

"Stop singing," a voice said from the backseat. "Your voice is terrible."

"What the-" Wesley was completely startled to find that he wasn't alone in his car and slammed on the brakes.

The car behind him squealed its tires to avoid hitting him.

"We're on the freeway, you idiot," the voice said. "Just drive."

Wesley hit the gas and continued forward in traffic, hoping that he hadn't caused an accident behind him.

He tried to look in his rearview mirror to see who exactly was in his backseat, but he couldn't see because of the sun coming in through the back window and blinding him in his mirror.

"Who are you?" Wesley said. "What do you want?"

"You're kidding me, right?" the voice said. "You don't recognize me, Wes?"

Wesley gripped the steering wheel tightly, twisting the fuzzy cover on the wheel in bizarre patterns as he tried to focus on the road. He liked the feel of the fluffy steering wheel cover. The tactile sensation helped to soothe his nerves in traffic. But at the present moment, it wasn't helping anything.

"I can't see you," Wesley said. "The sun is in my mirror."

"Oh, right, sorry," the voice said.

He felt someone climb past him from the backseat and into the passenger seat.

The creature was small, about three feet tall and fuzzy, like his steering wheel. The fuzz on the creature matched the blue of the steering wheel cover, and Wesley remembered why he chose the fuzzy steering wheel cover in the first place.

It reminded him of Tock. His imaginary childhood friend.

Wesley stared at the creature in the passenger seat. It was Tock, there was no doubt about it.

Tock was a light blue fuzzy rabbit-like creature. He had long talons on his paws and a face a bit more like a bear. But he had long ears and a fluffy tail like a bunny. But Wes had learned the hard way not to mention that.

Wesley tried to keep his eyes on the road, but he couldn't help but look back and forth between the car in front of him and the rabbit-like creature beside him.

Tock was definitely the worse for wear. His bib front jeans had holes and frayed edges all over. He looked dirty and banged up, like he had been dragged for quite a while. He was missing an eye and his face had large black yarn stitches that flattened down the blue fluffy hair on one cheek. The hair was worn on his feet, and it looked like he had lost half an ear.

"Keep your eyes on the road, Wes," Tock said. "I don't want to get in another accident."

"What accident were you in?" Wes asked. "You look terrible."

"Thanks a lot," Tock glared at him. "Since most of this is your fault."

"What?" Wes was surprised to hear the animosity in his old friend's voice. "My fault?"

"Yes, your fault," Tock said. "That's why I'm here."

"I don't understand," Wes said. "I haven't seen you in years."

"But you've been drawing me," Tock said. "Haven't you?"

"What?" Wes was so surprised that he almost forgot to watch the road. "How do you know about that?"

"You don't think I know everything that you've been up to?" Tock asked. "You don't think that I keep tabs on my best friend?"

"Keep tabs? How?" Wes asked. "I haven't seen you in years. Decades even."

"You don't think I know when my likeness is put down on paper?" Tock asked. "Even when you make me too much like a damn rabbit."

"Maybe I was just drawing a rabbit," Wes said, starting to feel a little defensive.

"No, it's not just a rabbit, it's me," Tock said. "You've been drawing me and our adventures. You may have changed my name, but it's me all the same."

"So?" Wes said. "I've finally gotten my big break because of it. They want to make a TV show out of you. Us. The character." Wes stammered through the last part of the sentence.

"And that is where the problem lies," Tock said. "I'm here to stop you from signing that contract."

"What? No!" Wes said. "Those are my adventures too. I can publish what I want."

"Wes, let me set you straight," Tock turned in the seat so that he was facing Wes with his back to the door. "There are some people that don't want our world exposed."

"People?" Wes asked. "What people?"

"People," Tock said. "Really more like monsters, or the powers-that-be."

"I don't understand," Wes said.

"You can't go around just exposing our world to your world," Tock said.

"No one is going to think it's real," Wes said. "It will be obvious to anyone who is sane that it is all imaginary."

"Imaginary to some is real to others," Tock said. "Your fantasy is my reality. Don't forget that."

"So, what are you going to do about it?" Wes asked. "You're a figment of my imagination."

Tock pulled out a gun and pointed it at Wes.

"I'm going to do whatever it takes to keep you from exposing all of us," Tock said. "If I don't, I'm next."

"Next what?" Wes asked. He looked over and eyed the handgun. "Is that real?"

Tock kept the gun low, with his ears tucked down so no one outside the car could see him in the passenger seat.

"It's real enough," Tock said. "Don't make me do something I will regret. I liked you. You were always good to me."

"Put the gun away," Wes said. "It's not real anyway. You and it are just a figment of my imagination. I must just be nervous about the meeting I am going to."

"Don't make me pull the trigger," Tock said. "Just get off at the next ramp, turn the car around, and head back home."

Wes laughed.

Tock raised the gun and pulled the trigger. The bullet whizzed past Wes's torso, under his arms, and ricocheted off the door with a loud ping.

"What the-?" Wes almost swerved into the next lane. "Are you insane?"

"Don't make me use this again," Tock said.

"That's a real effing gun?" Wes was stunned. "You almost shot me."

Wes raised his right hand to his left arm. There was blood, not a lot, but he was in too much shock to feel any pain.

"You hit me," Wes said.

"You caught some shrapnel," Tock said. "Sorry about that. It was just supposed to be a warning shot."

"You have a real friggen gun in my car and you shot me," Wes said.

"I didn't mean to," Tock said defensively. "It was the ricochet."

"I wouldn't have been hit by a ricochet if you hadn't fired a gun in my car," Wes yelled.

The woman in the next car over looked at Wes with a slightly horrified look on her face. She motioned to the driver of her car to go faster.

"Just get off the freeway," Tock said. "We can talk."

"I'm going to be late for my meeting," Wes said. "If I miss the meeting, I could lose the contract."

"That's why I'm here, knucklehead," Tock said. "To make sure you miss that meeting. Let's just do things the easy way and turn the car around and go home."

"You don't understand," Wes said. "Getting this gig could mean a lot of money."

Tock hesitated a moment.

"How much money?" Tock asked.

"A lot of money," Wes said again. "Movie spin-offs, more comic books, they already want to do a TV series."

Tock raised his head and looked out the windows of the car. He ducked back down before the driver in the next car saw him.

"Enough money to live on the run?" Tock asked.

"What do you mean?" Wes asked.

"I mean," Tock sort of bobbed his head from side to side. "If I let you do this, could we live on the run? Because certain people might not want any of our adventures to come to light."

"I-I don't know," Wes said. "I guess? Maybe? I don't know what they have in the contracts yet."

"Would you be willing to live somewhere else?" Tock cocked his head and looked up at Wes. He lowered the gun down into his lap and looked up at his old friend.

"What? Like another state?" Wes asked.

"No," Tock shook his head. "Like somewhere else entirely."

"What, like in Europe or something?" Wes looked down at his old friend in the passenger seat next to him.

Tock was lost in thought. But Wes recognized that face. It was the face that Tock made when he was planning something.

Something that usually wound up with both of them in a lot of trouble.

"No, I mean like another place entirely," Tock looked up at Wes. He rubbed his fuzzy blue chin with his paw. "Like where I'm from."

"You mean like another reality?' Wes looked to Tock again. He was having trouble concentrating on the road, but he really didn't want to die either. "Wouldn't that make it easier for the powers-that-be to find us?"

"No," Tock shook his head. His ears bobbled back and forth with the motion. "It would make it a thousand times harder."

"But wouldn't you get into trouble for taking a human there?" Wes asked.

"How much money do you think you could make if the adventures were in another place altogether?" Tock asked.

"What are you saying?" Wes asked.

"I'm saying that if you make it to that meeting, sign those contracts," Tock tapped the gun against his lap. "They're going to be after us, no matter where we go. So why not go on the run someplace that will make you even more money. Am I right?"

Tock looked up at Wes hopefully.

"I do miss our adventures together," Tock said.

Wes couldn't keep the smile from creeping across his face.

"They were asking if I had more ideas," Wes said. "For where the show might go in the future. I was supposed to have some pitches ready today."

"Do you think you can add some imagination to those pitches?" Tock asked.

"I think I can wing it," Wes smiled and looked out the windshield. He gripped the steering wheel with both hands and felt the familiar fuzz of the steering wheel cover helping to soothe his nerves.

Tock looked out the front windshield and then turned and squinted into the sun behind them.

"Well, my old friend," Tock said. "We have a meeting to get you to."

More books by Judy Lunsford:

The Bird Lady: 10th Anniversary Special Edition
Seeds of Today

The Portal Wars
The Grimoires

Gamers
Schemers

Fire Lily
Bezbell
Kirog

Moonlight Magic
Moonlight Melody

The Red Dart
Shadow Mountain
Crafting Christmas

For YA:
Life Unscripted
The Secret Gondal Society

Short Stories:
Dark of Night, The
Fairy Short Stories
Fairy Tales & Nightmares
Fantasy Faire
First Stories
Magic from the Dark
Story Hoard
The Wild Hunt

Thank you for reading.
If you enjoyed this book, you can find more stories
at
JudyLunsford.com
or your favorite online retailer.

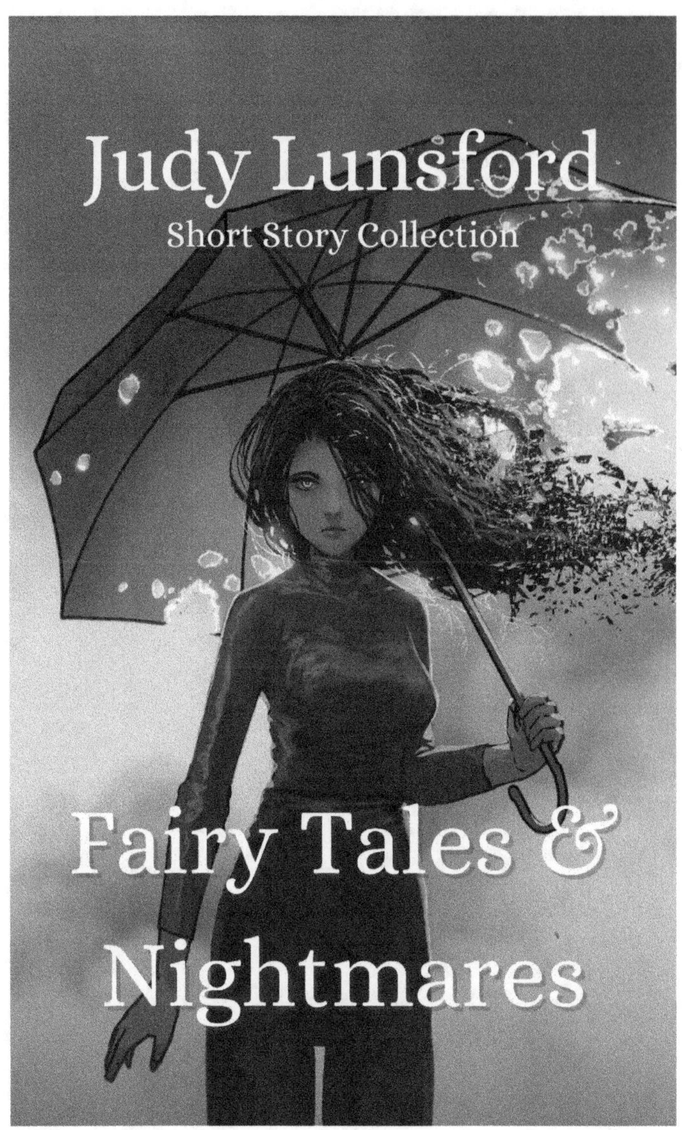

Judy Lunsford
Short Story Collection
Fairy Tales &
Nightmares

Short Story Collection
Magic from the Dark
Judy Lunsford

MONSTERS & REAPERS & GHOSTS, OH MY!
A SHORT STORY COLLECTION
JUDY LUNSFORD

Thank you for reading.

JudyLunsford.com